Vroom!

HOT SUVS

CADILLAC ESCALADE ESV PLATINUM

I0880322

Charles Piddock

Rourke Educational Media

rourkeeducationalmedia.com

TABLE OF CONTENTS

CADILLAC ESCALADE ESV PLATINUM

MEET THE BOSS

Who's the boss of the road? Who stands for power and beauty all wrapped up in one amazing package? The answer just might be the Cadillac Escalade ESV **Platinum**, or Esky, as its fans call it.

The Esky Platinum is much more than just another set of wheels. It's the top-of-the-line Cadillac SUV. Be warned: if you see this powerful beast on the road behind you, admire it. But also move over and let it pass.

The Esky ESV Platinum weighs 5,870 pounds (2,663 kilograms), yet can go from 0 to 60 miles (96.56 kilometers) per hour in only 6.1 seconds.

LOTS OF HORSES

The Esky Platinum looks powerful for good reason. Beneath its hood, like a sleeping tiger, purrs a big **V-8** engine. It produces 420 **horsepower** and 460 pound-feet (63.6 kilogram-meters) of **torque**. That gives the Esky about four times the horsepower and four times the torque as an average car. This muscle allows the Escalade ESV Platinum to tow up to 8,100 pounds (3,674 kilograms). That's as heavy as two full-size cars.

The best towing capacity for large SUVs is the Nissan Armada, which can pull up to 9,000 pounds (4,082 kilograms).

The Esky Platinum's engine looks sleek and smooth and hides a powerful V-8 engine.

A BEAST WITH BEAUTY

The Escalade ESV Platinum may be a beast, but it is also a beauty in its inside looks and cabin comfort. Soft lights illuminate its door handles. Its seats are heated for cold days and cooled for hot days. In addition, the Esky has a **massage** feature for its front seats. Press a button and the Esky's heated steering column will rise up to where you want it and tilt to where it is most comfortable.

The Esky ESV Platinum cabin also has **tri-zone** climate control. That means that just about everyone in the Esky is able to have their own heating and air conditioning.

Much of the interior of the Esky Platinum is covered with expensive leather. The seats are leather and the dashboard and door panels are leather.

SMOOTH AND SILENT

Despite its large size, the Esky's ride is both smooth and quiet. The secret is Cadillac's Magnetic Ride Control (MRC) **shock absorbers**. The Esky has magnetized fluids with sensors on each of its four wheels to pick up even the smallest changes in the surface of the road. Information instantly goes to an electronic control unit (ECU). This allows the ECU to adjust the SUV's ride to smooth out any bump in the road. The Esky also has a lot of little microphones around the cabin that cancel any outside sound from the road and the engine.

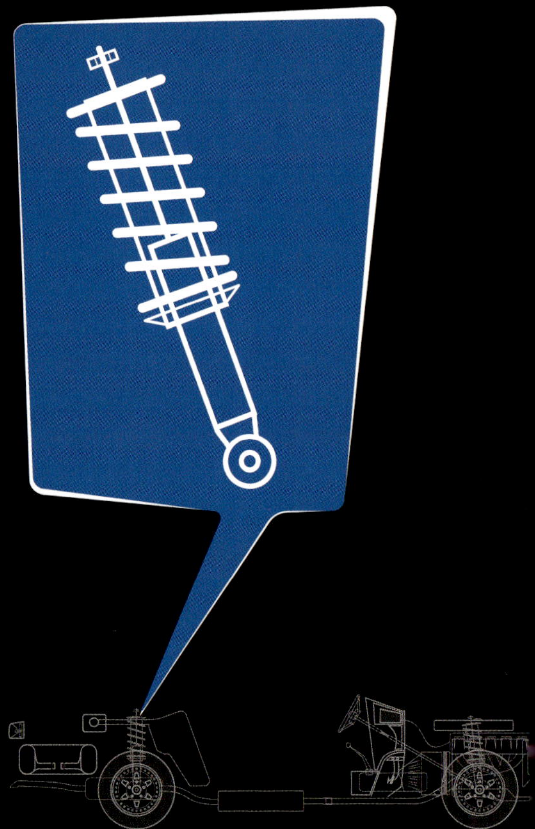

Shock absorbers are devices designed to eliminate the bumps caused by rough roads. Cars have a shock absorber on each wheel.

The Escalade ESV automatically adjusts its shock absorbers ten times faster than the blink of an eye!

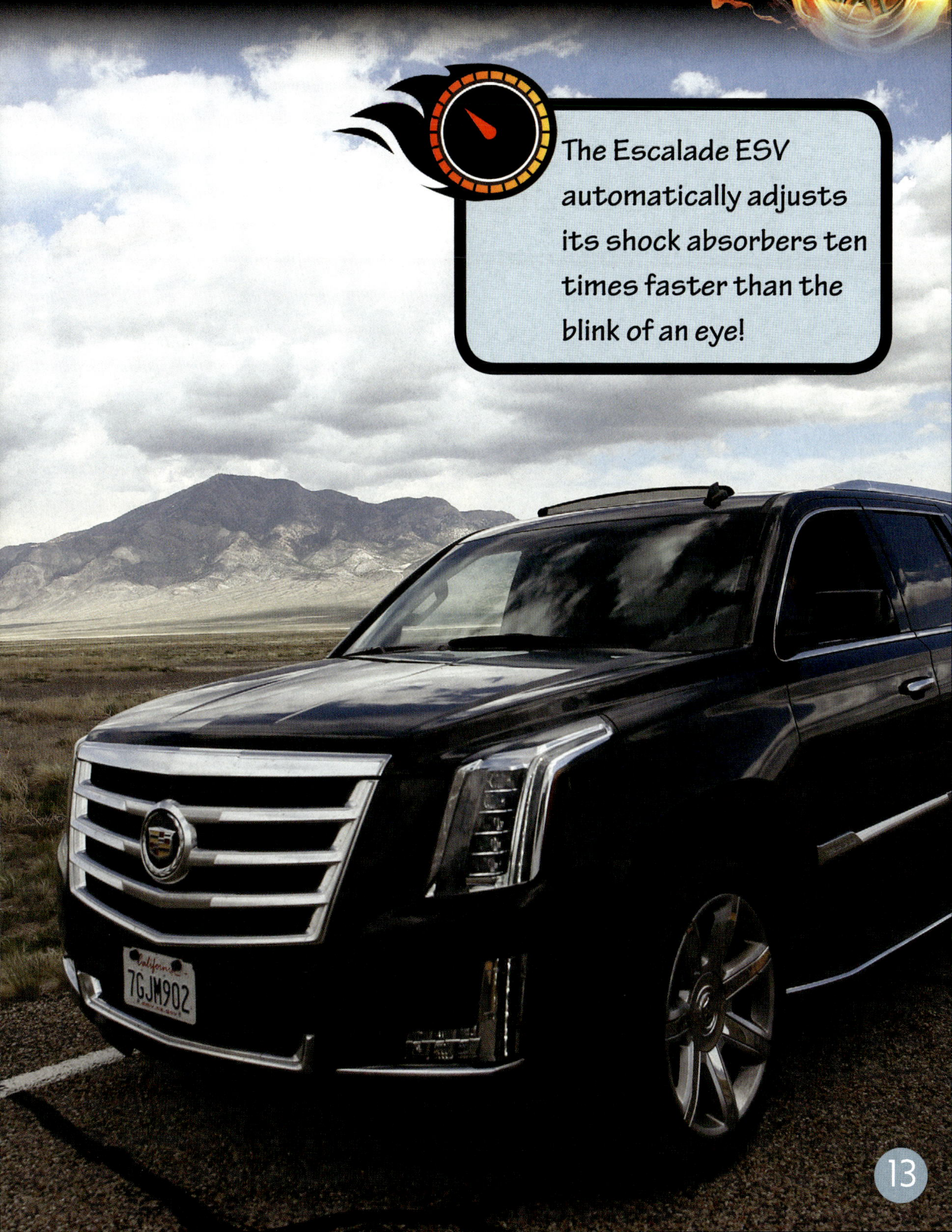

Rear Camera Mirror

Other features of the Esky Platinum include keyless **ignition**, or smart key, a hands-free power lift-gate, illuminated outside door handles, and heated outside mirrors.

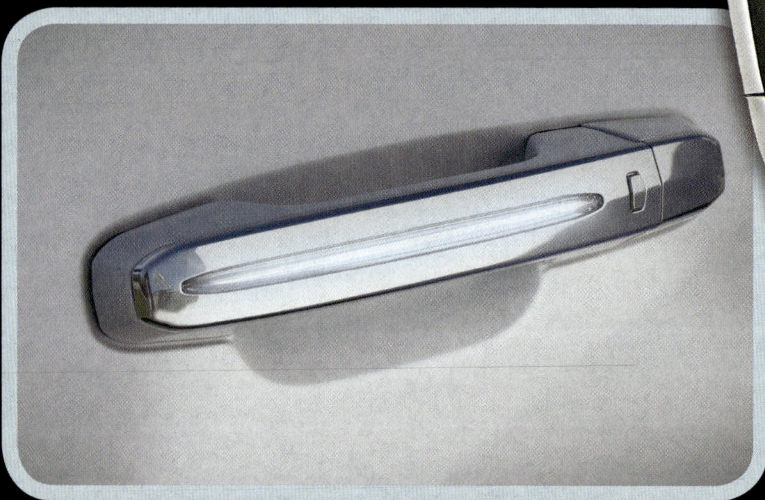

Illuminated handles and keyless ignition make it easier to locate and start the Esky at night.

The first keyless ignition was developed by Siemens in 1995, and introduced by Mercedes-Benz under the name "Key-less Go" in 1998 on the W220 S-Class, following its design patent filed by Daimler-Benz on May 17, 1997.

The Esky's rear camera mirror is an important safety device that allows drivers to see clearly behind them.

Introduced in 2017 for the Esky Platinum is the new hi-tech rear camera mirror. Utilizing a wide-angle camera mounted on the rear of the vehicle, the rear camera mirror system improves the field of vision in the mirror by an estimated 300 percent. That's about four times greater than through a normal rearview mirror.

STAYING CONNECTED

In the Cadillac Escalade ESV Platinum you can stay in touch even if you're in the middle of nowhere. Its dashboard screen connects the entire cabin to the Internet and to all important parts of the SUV inside and out. Wi-Fi is on whenever the car is turned on and it supports up to seven mobile phones and computers. The dashboard screen is so smart that it can recognize what you are about to touch even before you touch it. The system uses special sensors to activate automobile and electronic systems as the user's hand approaches the screen and dashboard.

The dashboard screen uses a technology called "capacitive sensing." Capacitive sensors work by generating an electric field. When this field is disrupted by your finger, for example, it signals the computer to do an action.

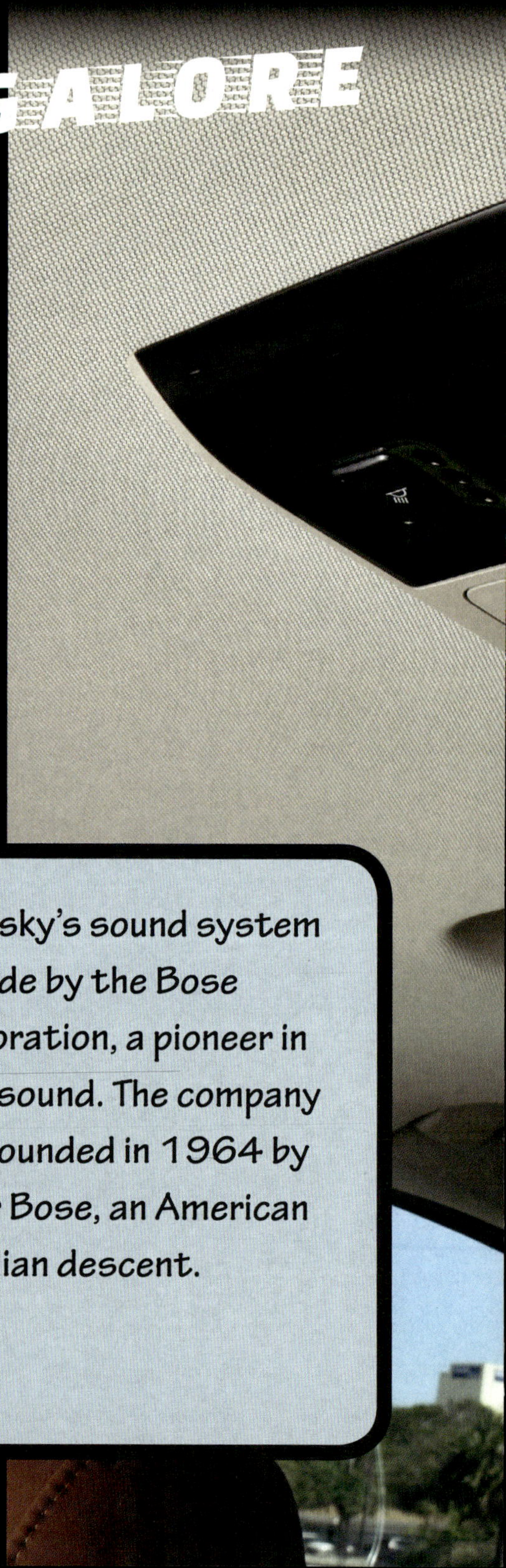

SPEAKERS GALORE

Traveling in an Esky is like sitting inside a music concert. Its surround sound system has 16 speakers. A DVD rear entertainment system includes two roof-mounted screens. The Esky also has electronic screens on the back of the front seat headrests.

The Esky's sound system is made by the Bose Corporation, a pioneer in auto sound. The company was founded in 1964 by Amar Bose, an American of Indian descent.

PUSH

Safety and Security

Short-range radar can prevent many common accidents and fender-benders.

The Esky's electronic marvels of course extend to active safety. It has front and rear automatic breaking that uses short-range **radar**. The radar senses a collision and automatically stops the vehicle. The Esky is also equipped with automatic parking assist. This uses special sensors to locate a parking space and automatically maneuver the car into it.

Radar is short for radio detection and ranging. Invented in the 1940s, radar sends out pulses of high-frequency waves that are reflected off an object, such as another car, and back to its source.

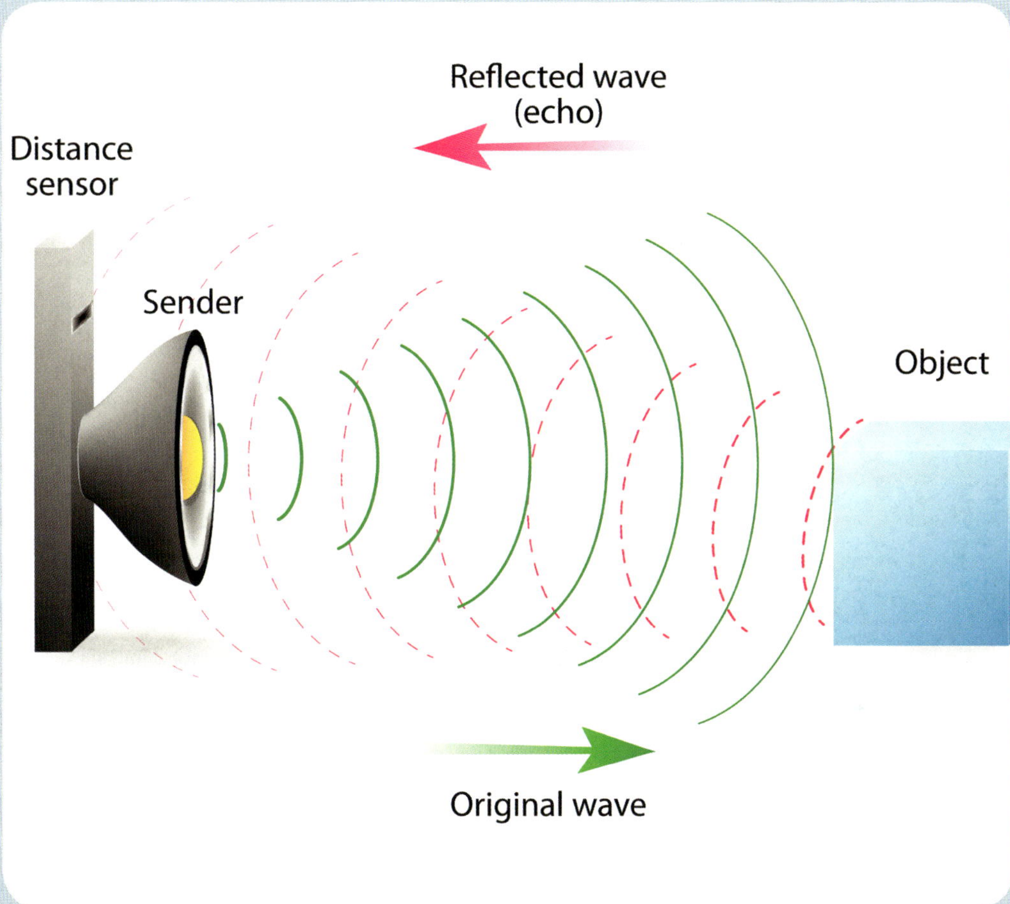

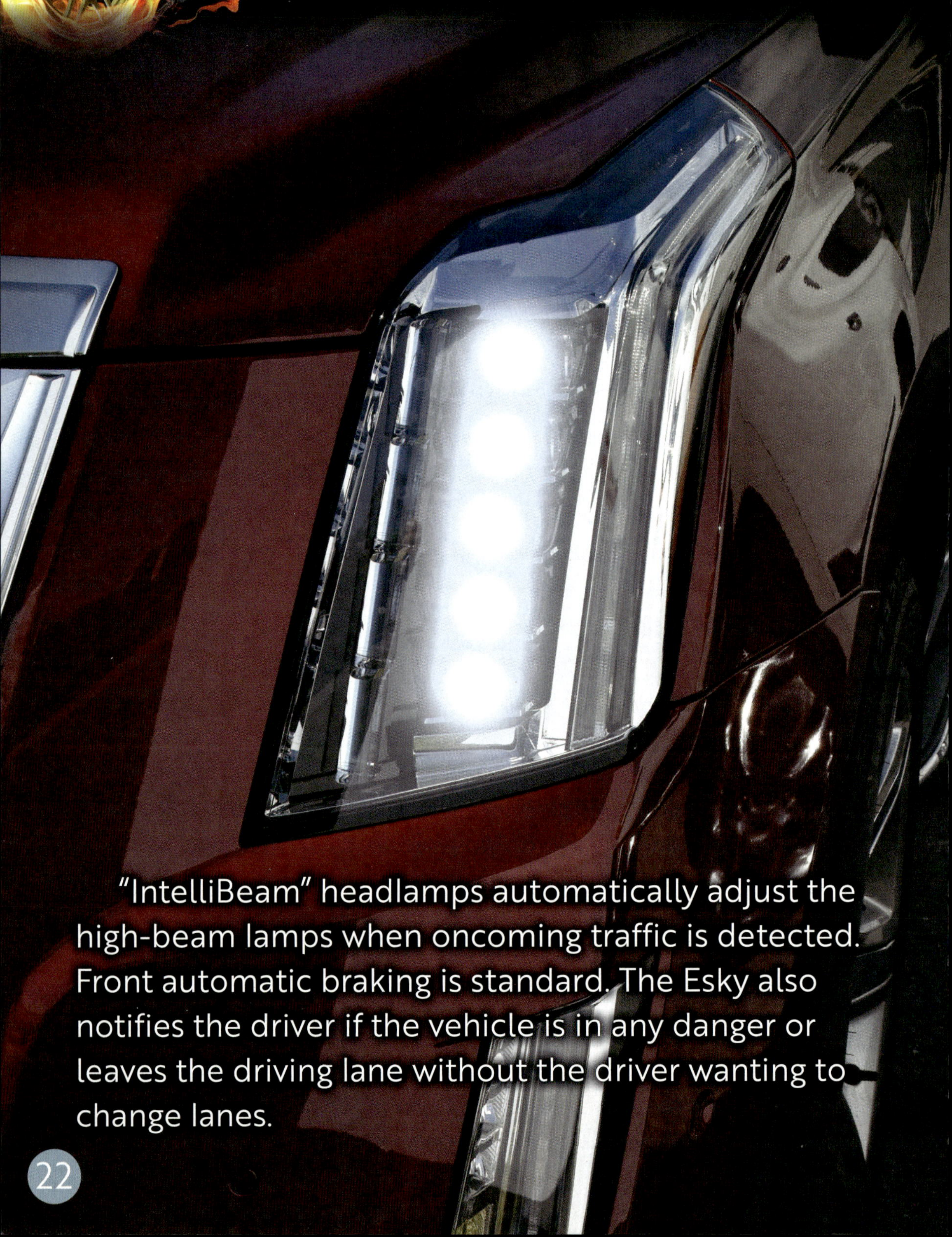

"IntelliBeam" headlamps automatically adjust the high-beam lamps when oncoming traffic is detected. Front automatic braking is standard. The Esky also notifies the driver if the vehicle is in any danger or leaves the driving lane without the driver wanting to change lanes.

The first electric headlamps were introduced in 1898 on the Columbia Electric Car from the Electric Vehicle Company of Hartford, Connecticut, and were optional!

The Cadillac Story

Cadillac is among the oldest automobile brands in the world. The company was named after French explorer Antoine Laumet de La Mothe, sieur de Cadillac, who founded Detroit in 1701. Cadillac's first two automobile models, the Runabout and Tonneau, were completed in October 1902.

Top photo: The 1904 Cadillac was also adapted as a delivery vehicle.

Right: The 1908 Cadillac was considered the top of the line for its time.

They were two-seat horseless carriages powered by a 10 horsepower single-cylinder engine. The company also emphasized **stylish** luxury finishes, causing its cars to be ranked among the finest in the United States. In 1912, Cadillac was the first automobile maker to use an electrical system for starting, ignition, and lighting.

Cadillac was purchased by General Motors (GM) in 1909. From the 1910 Cadillac Model S to the 1931 Cadillac Phaeton to the 1940 Cadillac 90 Town Car, Cadillacs were the favorite car of the rich and famous. On November 25, 1949, Cadillac produced its one-millionth car.

Tailfins were first added in 1948, growing in size until 1960. They disappeared in the 1965 model year.

In the 1950s, tailfins were considered the height of coolness in car styles.

In 1954 Cadillac was the first automaker to provide power steering and automatic windshield washers as standard equipment on all its vehicles. The Escalade made its first appearance in 1999.

During World War II (1939—45), Cadillac produced tanks and airplane engines for the U.S. war effort.

The 1965 Cadillac was long and luxurious.

LOOK MA, NO HANDS

The 2018 Escalade ESV Platinum features Cadillac's SuperCruise. SuperCruise is the world's first true hands-free driving system for highways. Once the driver turns on SuperCruise, the Esky takes over, keeping the vehicle at a constant speed, slowing down when approaching another car, speeding up when passing. Even though the driver doesn't touch the steering wheel, they must pay attention. Special software tracks the driver's head and automatically alerts them when their eyes aren't on the road. If the steering wheel light bar flashes green, the system has detected that the driver may not be paying attention.

One step beyond SuperCruise is a completely self-driving car. A self-driving car is one that is capable of sensing its environment and navigating without human input at all.

If the steering wheel light bar flashes green for too long, SuperCruise will alert the driver to take control of the steering immediately by flashing the light bar red. If the steering wheel light bar flashes red for too long, a voice command will tell the driver to take control of the vehicle. Continued failure to take over steering will cause the vehicle to slow to a stop. The brake lights and hazard warning flashers will then come on, and an emergency advisor will be called.

GM is developing a fleet of self-driving cars called the Chevrolet Bolt. In the next couple of years GM hopes to have a number of Bolts in cities able to pick up passengers and deliver them to a destination without human intervention.

GLOSSARY

horsepower (HORS-pou-ur): a unit for measuring the power of an engine

ignition (ig-NISH-uhn): the activation of an engine by means of an electrical spark

massage (muh-SAHZH): use of vibration or rubbing to cause muscles to relax

platinum (PLAT-uh-nuhm): a very valuable silvery-white metal (name used by Cadillac to indicate the top-of-the-line Escalade)

radar (RAY-dahr): a way ships, planes and other vehicles find solid objects by reflecting radio waves off them and by receiving the reflected waves

shock absorbers (shahk ab-ZORB-erz): devices that attach to a car's wheels to lessen the effect of a rough road

stylish (STY-lish): displaying the latest style, fashionable

torque (tork): a twisting force that causes rotation

tri-zone (try-zohn): covering each of three areas, as in tri-zone heating or cooling

V-8 (Vee-ate): an eight-cylinder gasoline engine with the cylinders organized like the letter V

INDEX

SHOW WHAT YOU KNOW

1. How many pounds is the Esky able to tow?
2. What is the main advantage of tri-zone climate control?
3. What enables the Esky to have automatic braking?
4. Who was the Cadillac car company named for?
5. In what year did Cadillac first produce an Escalade?

FURTHER READING

Arnold, Nick, *How Cars Work: The Interactive Guide to Mechanisms That Make a Car Move*, Running Press, 2013.

Colson, Rob, *Top Marques: SUVs and Off Roaders:* Wayland Publishers, 2016.

Zink, Bradley, *It Starts with a Key: How Cars Work:* CreateSpace Independent Publishing Platform, 2016.

ABOUT THE AUTHOR

Charles Piddock is the former Editor-in-Chief of Weekly Reader Corporation. He has written many books for both young people and adults. He and his wife live by a lake in south-central Maine.

Meet The Author!
www.meetREMauthors.com

© 2019 Rourke Educational Media

All rights reserved. No part of this book may be reproduced or utilized in any form or by any means, electronic or mechanical including photocopying, recording, or by any information storage and retrieval system without permission in writing from the publisher.

www.rourkeeducationalmedia.com

PHOTO CREDITS: All photos © Blue Door Education except cover © GM Co.; pages 4-5 © Brphoto | Dreamstime.com and 13 © © Kanison | Dreamstime.com., page 12 illustration © Denys Po/Shutterstock.com, page 17 map on screen © scanrail/istockphoto.com, page 19 cartoon on screen © artisticco/istockphoto, page 21 © Designua/Dreamstime, page 23 courtesy Beaulieu National Motor Museum, page 24 © svlambo https://creativecommons.org/licenses/by/2.0/deed.en; page 24 1904 Cadillac with delivery body public domain; page 26 © Christer Johansson https://creativecommons.org/licenses/by-sa/2.5/deed.en; page 29 © Grzegorz Czapski / Shutterstock.com

Edited by: Keli Sipperley

Cover design by Rhea Magaro-Wallace Interior design by: Nicola Stratford www.nicolastratford.com

Library of Congress PCN Data

Cadillac Escalade ESV Platinum / Charles Piddock
(*VROOM!* Hot SUVs)
ISBN 978-1-64156-475-5 (hard cover)
ISBN 978-1-64156-601-8 (soft cover)
ISBN 978-1-64156-715-2 (e-Book)
Library of Congress Control Number: 2018930693

Rourke Educational Media
Printed in the United States of America, North Mankato, Minnesota